Successories®

Great Little Book on The Gift of Self-Confidence

By
Brian Tracy

CAREER PRESS
3 Tice Road, P.O. Box 68
Franklin Lakes, NJ 07417
1-800-CAREER-1; 201-848-0310 (NJ and outside U.S.)
FAX: 201-848-1727

SUCCESSORIES®: GREAT LITTLE BOOK ON THE GIFT OF SELF-CONFIDENCE
ISBN 1-56414-330-9, $6.99 / Cover design by Jenmar Graphics
Typesetting by Eileen Munson
Printed in the U.S.A. by Book-mart Press

To order this title by mail, please include price as noted above, $2.50 handling per order, and $1.50 for each book ordered. Send to: Career Press, Inc., 3 Tice Road, P.O. Box 687, Franklin Lakes, NJ 07417. Or call toll-free 1-800-CAREER-1 (NJ and Canada: 201-848-0310) to order using VISA or MasterCard, or for further information on books from Career Press.

Library of Congress Catalog Card Number: 97-75076

Self-confidence is the foundation of all great success and achievement.

You can accomplish anything that you put your mind to, if you want it badly enough.

Average people have wishes and hopes. Confident people have goals and plans.

Ask yourself, "What one great thing would I dare to dream if I knew I could not fail?"

>—◊—<

It is not lack of ability or opportunity that holds you back; it is only a lack of confidence in yourself.

>—◊—<

There are no limits to what you can accomplish, except the limits you place on your own thinking.

Confidence is a habit that can be developed by acting as if you already had the confidence you desire to have.

Imagine no limitations. What would you do with your life if you had all the education, experience, and resources that you require?

How would you change your life if you won $1 million cash today? Whatever your answer, start today to take those actions.

Dream big dreams! Only big dreams have the power to move your mind and spirit.

The key to self-confidence is for you to decide what you want and then act as if it were impossible to fail.

➤—◊—◀

"Boldness has genius, power and magic in it."
—Goethe

➤—◊—◀

Idealize! Define the ideal future vision of your life in every detail.

Fear and doubt are the major enemies of great success and achievement.

>—◇—<

The first part of the word "triumph" is "try."

>—◇—<

The future belongs to the *askers*. Resolve today to ask for what you want in every area of your life.

What are you doing today that, knowing what you now know, you wouldn't get into again if you had to do it over?

You are always free to choose what you do more of, what you do less of, and what you do not at all.

Self-confident people do not compare themselves to others. They only compare themselves with the very best that they can be.

Commit yourself to excellence in every part of your life and never stop striving toward it.

Do what you love to do and put your whole heart into becoming good at it.

When you meet other people, look them in the eye, state your name clearly, and shake hands firmly.

The way you give your name to others is a measure of how much you like and respect yourself.

An attitude of positive self-expectancy is a great builder of confidence.

Expect to be successful, expect to be liked, expect to be popular everywhere you go.

You are nature's greatest miracle. There never has been and never will be anyone just like you.

You do not need to be different from who you are. You only need to be *more* of the person you already are.

Define your life in your own terms and live every minute consistent with the very best person you can possibly be.

There is no problem you cannot solve, no obstacle you cannot overcome, and no goal you cannot achieve.

Anything anyone else has done, you can probably do as well, if you want to badly enough.

No one is better than you—some people are just better developed and more knowledgeable in certain areas.

In sales and business, the future belongs to the askers—the people who ask for what they want, over and over.

Define your ideal lifestyle in every respect. What could you do today to begin creating it?

"If a thing is worth doing, it is worth doing badly."
—G. K. Chesterton

Anything worth doing is worth doing poorly at first, until you master it.

You can learn anything you need to learn to achieve any goal you can set for yourself.

Your mind is like a muscle—the more you use it, the more powerful it becomes.

Intelligence is a way of acting. If you act intelligently you are smart, regardless of your IQ.

You develop confidence by acting confidently and courageously when you could just as well play it safe.

Confident people think, decide, and then take action. Be decisive!

Accept complete responsibility for every part of your life. Refuse to blame others or make excuses.

Accept that you are where you are and what you are because of yourself. If you don't like it, change it!

Face your problems squarely. As Shakespeare said, "Take arms against a sea of troubles, and in so doing, end them."

Fake it until you make it! Act as if you had all the confidence you require until it becomes your reality.

Become an unshakable optimist—look for the good in every situation.

>—◇—<

Within every difficulty you face, there lies the seed of an equal or greater opportunity or benefit.

>—◇—<

Seek for the valuable lesson in every setback or disappointment—you will always find one.

After every difficulty, ask yourself two questions: "What did I do right?" and "What would I do differently?"

The greatest human quality is that of becoming unstoppable! And you become unstoppable by refusing to quit, no matter what happens.

Talk to yourself positively all the time. Keep repeating, "I can do it! I can do it!" until your fears disappear.

"Do the thing you fear and the death of fear is certain."
—Ralph Waldo Emerson

Self-doubt does more to sabotage individual potential than all external limitations put together.

Decide today to be a *master* of change rather than a *victim* of change.

The best way to predict your future is for you to create it.

Self-confidence is a learnable skill, like typing or riding a bicycle. You develop it with practice.

Develop high levels of self-confidence by acting as if you already had them.

Decide exactly what you want and resolve to persist, no matter what, until you achieve it.

Building self-confidence is like building muscle—you start with the basic structure and then you build on it.

You are far more intelligent and creative than you realize. Resolve to get smarter and sharper every day.

You can achieve almost any goal if you just do what other successful people have done to achieve the same goals before you.

The key to success is for you to make a habit throughout your life of doing the things you fear.

"If you do not do the thing you fear, the fear controls your life."
—Glenn Ford, American actor

Everyone is afraid. The superior person is the one who acts in spite of his fears.

If you were totally unafraid of failure, what goals would you set for yourself?

If you did not care at all about what anyone else thought about you, what would you do differently, or change in your life?

Don't ever worry about what people might think.
Other people aren't really thinking about you at all!

You become what you think about most of the time.
Think about what you want rather than what you
don't want.

You are a thoroughly good person—negative ideas you have about yourself have no basis in reality.

Think about your goals all the time.

Clear written goals with plans of action will build your self-confidence as fast as any other factor.

"Believe in yourself; every heart vibrates to that iron string."
—Ralph Waldo Emerson

You are in an ongoing process of becoming, growing, and developing in the direction of your dominant thoughts. What are they?

Whatever you think about grows in your life.

➤—◆—◄

Your thought is creative. Thoughts held in mind, produce after their kind.

➤—◆—◄

Self-confident people think and talk about what they really want—and they tend to get it.

Whatever you believe with conviction becomes your reality. Choose your beliefs with care.

➤—◇—◄

Challenge your self-limiting beliefs. Most of them are not true at all.

➤—◇—◄

Confidence comes from living your life in harmony with the very best that you know.

Confidence on the outside begins by living with integrity on the inside.

>—◊—<

Be absolutely clear about who you are and what you stand for. Refuse to compromise.

>—◊—<

The more you do of what you're doing, the more you'll get of what you've got.

You always evolve and develop in the direction of your dominant aspirations and your innermost convictions.

You experience calmness and confidence when you know you are doing the right thing—whatever it costs.

"To thine own self be true and then it must follow, as the night the day, thou canst not then be false to any man."
—Shakespeare

Your self-confidence increases when you know you are living your life according to your highest values.

What would you do, how would you change your life, if you learned today that you only had six months to live?

Companies with clear written statements of values and principles are more dynamic and profitable than those without. People, too.

What are your values? What do you stand for and believe in?

>—◊—◄

You can always tell your true values by looking at your behavior—especially under pressure.

>—◊—◄

Who you are on the inside is always reflected by what you do on the outside.

What is your vision for yourself and your life?
Where do you want to be in five years?

A clear vision, backed by definite plans, gives you a tremendous feeling of confidence and personal power.

People ignore what you say. They are only concerned with what you *do*.

➤—◆—◄

The only measure of whether you truly believe something is how consistently you practice it.

➤—◆—◄

Live your life in every way to earn and keep the respect of the people *you* respect.

Self-confident people are very clear about who they are and what they believe in.

Integrity is more than a value—it is the quality that guarantees all the other values.

Determine your unifying principles in life and resolve to live by them.

Unshakable self-confidence comes from unshakable commitment to your values.

If you were to write out your own obituary or eulogy, what would you want it to say about you after you die?

Happiness and self-confidence come naturally when you feel yourself moving and progressing toward becoming the very best person you can possibly be.

Organize your values by priority. What is more important to you? What is less important?

Set peace of mind as your highest goal and organize your entire life around it.

When you listen to your "inner voice" and follow your intuition, you will probably never make another mistake.

Resolve today to either resolve or walk away from any situation that makes you unhappy or causes you stress.

"People are just about as happy as they make up their minds to be."
—Abraham Lincoln

Denial is the root source of most mental illness.
What is it in your life that you're not facing?

Self-confidence comes naturally when your inner
life and your outer life are in harmony.

Deal with life the way it is, not the way you wish
it could be.

Accept yourself as a valuable and worthwhile person in every respect.

Speak about yourself in positive and constructive terms only. Never sell yourself short.

Intensity of purpose and commitment to a single goal or objective builds your self-confidence.

High levels of self-confidence require that you always choose to live by a higher-order value rather than a lower-order value.

The most important values in life are contained in the people you love and the people who love you.

Every act of self-discipline increases your confidence, trust, and belief in yourself and your abilities.

"Self-confidence is the ability to make yourself do what you should do, when you should do it, whether you feel like it or not."
—Elbert Hubbard, author and lecturer

The great riches of life are self-esteem, self-respect, and personal pride—all based on self-confidence.

Persistence in the face of adversity builds your self-confidence and your ability to persist even more.

Persistence is self-discipline in action.

Every act of self-discipline and persistence increases your levels of self-esteem, self-respect, and personal pride.

The natural tendency of all human behavior is toward the path of least resistance. When you resist this tendency, you become stronger and more powerful.

Persisting through lesser difficulties builds your capacity to persist through greater difficulties, and achieve even greater things.

"Our great fear is not that we are powerless, but that we are powerful beyond measure."
—Nelson Mandela, South African leader

People with self-confidence set big goals for themselves in every area of life.

Setting big goals for yourself increases your confidence and your belief that they are attainable.

Write out your major goals, in the present tense, every single day.

Every time you write out a goal, it increases your confidence that the goal is achievable for you.

➤—◊—◄

Self-confidence is an attitude and attitudes are more important than facts.

➤—◊—◄

"Are you denying your greatness?"
—Les Brown, motivational speaker

Your life is a reflection of your thoughts. If you change your thinking, you change your life.

Visualize, imagine yourself as the calm, confident powerful person you really are inside.

Think positively. The more optimistic you are, the more confident you become.

The more confident you are, the more you attract into your life people and circumstances that can help you to achieve your goals.

To build your confidence, repeat over and over, "I feel happy! I feel healthy! I feel terrific!"

Single-minded concentration toward your major goal gives you a sense of power, purpose, and self-direction.

Clarity is essential. Knowing exactly what you want builds your self-confidence immeasurably.

What have you always wanted to do but been afraid to attempt? Whatever it is, it may be your greatest opportunity in life.

Cast aside your doubts. Make a total commitment to living the life you were meant to live.

The depth of your belief and the strength of your conviction determines the power of your personality.

A feeling of confidence and personal power comes from facing challenges and overcoming them.

The foundation of confidence in virtually every field is preparation.

>—◇—<

The more you learn and know in any area, the more confident you are.

>—◇—<

Overlearning and overpreparing gives you the winning edge in any area.

The comfort zone is the great enemy of courage and confidence.

"There is no security in life, only opportunity."
—General Douglas McArthur

Learn something new. Try something different. Convince yourself that you have no limits.

What appears to be your biggest problem in life may disguise your greatest opportunity.

You have within you, right now, the ability to be, have, and do far more than you've ever dreamed before.

You have been put on this earth to do something wonderful with your life.

The single common denominator of men and women who achieve great things is a sense of destiny.

"Compared to what we could be, we are only half awake. We are making use of only a small part of our physical and mental resources. Stating the thing broadly, the human individual thus lives far within his limits. He possesses powers of various sorts which he habitually fails to use."
—William James, American philosopher

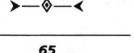

Imagine there were no limitations on what you could be, have, or do in any area of life. What goals would you set for yourself?

>—◇—<

Decide what's right before you decide what's possible.

>—◇—<

Goals in writing are dreams with deadlines.

There are no unrealistic goals—only unrealistic deadlines.

Committing your goals to paper increases the likelihood of your achieving them by 1,000 percent!

Make every goal clear, specific, measurable, and time bounded.

The foundation of lasting self-confidence and self-esteem is excellence, mastery of your work.

"The power which resides in man is new in nature, and none but he knows what that is which he can do, nor does he know until he has tried."
—Ralph Waldo Emerson

The outer limit of your potential is determined solely by your own beliefs and your own confidence in what you think is possible.

The better you are at what you do, the more you like yourself and the greater is your self-confidence.

Be a lifelong student. The more you learn, the more you earn and the more self-confidence you have.

>—◇—<

A motto for lasting self-confidence is, "Get good, get better, be the best!"

>—◇—<

You will only be truly happy and self-confident when you know you are really good at what you do.

What can you, and only you, do that if done well, will make a real difference in your life?

>—◆—<

What is your "heart's desire?" What are you really meant to do with your life?

>—◆—<

Don't hold grudges. Refuse to blame anyone for anything that has happened in your life.

Accepting total responsibility for your life gives you a tremendous feeling of personal power and self-confidence.

Forgive everyone who has ever hurt you in any way. Let it go.

What activities, behaviors, or decisions have been most responsible for your success in life? Do more of them.

Do more than you are paid for. There are never any traffic jams on the extra mile.

Your success in life will be in direct proportion to what you do after you do what you are expected to do.

Resolve to pay any price or make any sacrifice to get into the top 10 percent in your field. The payoff is incredible!

Every great success is an accumulation of thousands of ordinary efforts that no one sees or appreciates.

➤—◇—◀

Everything counts! Everything you do helps or hurts, adds up or takes away.

➤—◇—◀

The harder you work, the luckier you get, and the more self-confidence you have.

There are no shortcuts. To be a big success, start a little earlier, work a little harder, and stay a little later.

"Do what you can, with what you have, right where you are."
—Theodore Roosevelt

You have the capacity to become very, very good in anything that is really important to you.

What one skill, if you developed it and did it in an excellent fashion, would have the greatest positive impact on your career?

A feeling of continuous growth is a wonderful source of motivation and self-confidence.

Read an hour every day in your chosen field. This works out to about one book per week, 50 books per year, and will guarantee your success.

Invest 3 percent of your income back into yourself in the form of continuous learning.

Listen to audio programs in your car. This works out to 500 to1,000 hours per year of high-quality education—better than attending university.

You are your most valuable asset. Take all the training you can get to increase your value.

Continuous learning is the minimum requirement for success in your field.

High levels of competence and mastery in your field will give you a feeling of unshakable self-confidence.

There is nothing that can stop you from getting to the top of your field—except yourself.

Get around the right people. Associate with positive, goal-oriented people who encourage and inspire you.

Self-confidence requires high levels of health and energy.

"Fatigue doth make cowards of us all."
—Vince Lombardi, football coach

Take control over your environment and ensure that it is predominantly positive.

Feed your mind with healthy, nutritious intellectual protein, not mental candy.

Be selective about what you see, watch, hear, and listen to. Keep your external influences predominantly positive.

Television can be a wonderful tool or a terrible master, depending on what you watch, and how you watch it.

See and think of yourself as a leader and then do what leaders do. Dare to go forward.

Be a *creator* of circumstances rather than just a *creature* of circumstances. Be proactive rather than reactive.

A sense of control is essential to a feeling of self-confidence and a positive mental attitude.

Take complete control over the messages you allow into your conscious mind.

Control your inner dialogue. Talk to yourself positively all the time.

Visualize and think about yourself as you would ideally *like* to be, not just as you are.

It is not what happens to you, but how you respond to what happens to you that determines how you feel.

Decide in advance to respond positively and constructively to every adversity.

Develop an attitude of positive self-expectancy, confidently expecting to gain something from every situation.

Happiness is the progressive realization of a worthy goal or ideal. Do something to move toward your goals every single day.

Avoid negative people at all costs. They are the greatest destroyers of self-confidence and self-esteem.

If your happiness is dependent on someone changing, you are bound to be disappointed.

Confident people are willing to take risks; people who take risks develop self-confidence.

Single-minded concentration in the direction of your dreams intensifies your desires and increases your self-confidence.

"Don't ask for things to be easier; ask instead for you to be better."
—Jim Rohn, success philosopher

The better you get along with other people, the better you feel about yourself.

Most of your happiness will come from your relationships with others. Handle them with care.

The more you like and respect yourself, the more you like and respect others, and the more they like and respect you.

The more you do for others without expectation of return, the more you'll get back from the most unexpected sources.

Your self-confidence is directly connected to how much you feel you are making a difference in your world.

Whenever you do something nice for someone else, your self-esteem and self-confidence go up proportionately.

The best words for resolving a disagreement are, "I could be wrong; I often am." It's true.

Practice the body language of self-confidence. Stand tall and straight with your chin high and walk briskly. You will feel better and act better.

Make others feel important. The more important you make them feel, the more important you feel, as well.

Treat each person with consideration, caring and courtesy—and watch your confidence soar!

➤—◆—◄

Everytime you say "thank you" to another person, they feel better and so do you.

➤—◆—◄

Develop an "attitude of gratitude:" Be thankful for every good thing in your life.

Everything that you do or say that raises the self-esteem of another raises yours as well.

Your self-confidence will be determined by the people you surround yourself with as much as by any other factor.

Total commitment to a relationship builds your confidence and self-esteem.

Complete acceptance of yourself as a valuable and worthwhile person is a real self-esteem builder.

Everyone earns their living by selling something to someone. How good are you?

Your ability to persuade and influence others determines the quality of your life, and your self-confidence.

The more effective you are with people, the calmer and more confident you will feel.

Learning to speak in public will increase your self-confidence dramatically.

>—◇—<

Life is too short to waste a minute of it doing a job you don't like or care about.

>—◇—<

Confidence comes from being prepared to cut your losses, to walk away from a bad situation.

If you were not doing your current job today, would you apply for it? Would you get it?

The ideal job for you is usually easy to learn and easy to do. You can hardly wait to get there.

If you don't want to be excellent at your current job, it's probably not the right job for you.

Where do you want to be in five years? Is what you are doing right now going to get you there?

High levels of self-confidence comes from the feeling that you are the master of your own destiny.

Learn to negotiate in your best interests. It makes you feel terrific.

Be a great listener. Ask questions and listen intently to the answers.

>—◇—◂

Determine your personal *Area of Excellence*. How can you best capitalize on it.

>—◇—◂

Choose a field you enjoy and then become totally absorbed in it.

Self-confidence requires having the courage to live your life in your own way.

"Courage is rightly considered the foremost of the virtues, for upon it, all others depend."
—Winston Churchill

Be prepared to reinvent yourself every year. Imagine starting over with no limitations or encumbrances.

You have far more weaknesses than strengths —concentrate always on your strengths.

Concentrate on one thing, the most important thing, and stay with it until it's complete.

Think on paper. Set priorities and always work on your highest-value tasks.

Self-confidence comes when you are working at peak levels of efficiency and effectiveness.

The more high-value tasks you accomplish, the more powerful and positive you feel.

In times of turbulence and rapid change, you must constantly be re-evaluating yourself relative to the new realities.

Keep setting new and higher goals and standards for yourself. Never be satisfied.

You can accomplish virtually anything if you want it badly enough and if you are willing to work long enough and hard enough.

A feeling of significance arises in you when you know that you are making a difference in the world.

Never settle for anything less than your best.

"Persistence is to the character of man as carbon is to steel."
—Napoleon Hill, success author and expert

Your ability to function well in the inevitable crisis is the true measure of the person you are.

Life is a continuous succession of problems. The only question is how you respond to them.

You can develop any quality that you desire to achieve any goal that you set for yourself.

What is your *Limiting Step?* What is holding you back from the life you desire?

Work at least as hard on yourself as you do on your job.

You have more talent and ability than you could ever use in an entire lifetime.

Desire is the only real limit on your abilities.

"There are powers inside of you, which, if you could discover and use, would make of you everything you ever dreamed or imagined you'd become."
—Orison Swett Marden, success author

Act boldly, and unseen forces will come to your aid.

When you want something badly enough, you will develop the confidence and the ability to overcome any obstacle in your way.

Resolve in advance to persist until you succeed, no matter what the difficulty.

To keep yourself positive and self-confident, think about your goals all the time.

Flood your mind with positive words, images, books, tapes, and conversations.

If you can dream it, you can do it. Your limits are all within yourself.

"Do you want to be successful faster? Then double your rate of failure."
—Thomas J. Watson, Sr., founder of IBM

Successful people make a habit of decisiveness in everything they do.

There is nothing wrong with making mistakes. Learning from mistakes is how we grow.

➤—◈—◄

When you absolutely believe in yourself and your ability to succeed, nothing will stop you.

➤—◈—◄

Success comes in *cans*, not in *can'ts*.

The Law of Cause and Effect is the iron law of human destiny. Thoughts are causes, and conditions are effects.

Your level of optimism is determined by how you explain things to yourself. Think positively.

Make a game of finding something positive in every situation—95 percent of your emotions are determined by how you interpret events to yourself.

Carpe diem. Seize the day! Do the thing and you will have the power.

"Courage is not absence of fear, lack of fear. It is control of fear, mastery of fear."
—Mark Twain

The history of the human race is the history of ordinary people who have overcome their fears and accomplished extraordinary things.

To discover new continents, you must be willing to lose sight of the shore.

>—◈—◄

Failure is an indispensable prerequisite for success. It is how you learn the lessons you need.

>—◈—◄

Remember, you only have to succeed the last time.

Live in truth with all people under all circumstances.

➤—◈—◄

Continually set higher standards for yourself,
knowing confidently that you can reach them.

➤—◈—◄

Whatever you can do, or dream you can, begin it.

"If a man advances confidently in the direction of his dreams, he will experience a success unknown in common times."
—Henry David Thoreau, American philosopher

About the author

Brian Tracy is a world authority on the development of human potential and personal effectiveness. He teaches his key ideas, methods, and techniques on peak performance to more than 100,000 people every year, showing them how to double and triple their productivity and get their lives into balance at the same time. This book contains some of the best concepts ever discovered.

These other Successories® titles are available from Career Press:

- ▶ *Great Little Book for The Peak Performance Woman*
- ▶ *Great Little Book on Effective Leadership*
- ▶ *Great Little Book on Mastering Your Time*

- ▶ *Great Little Book on Personal Achievement*
- ▶ *Great Little Book on Successful Selling*
- ▶ *Great Little Book on Universal Laws of Success*
- ▶ *Great Quotes from Great Women*
- ▶ *Great Quotes from Great Sports Heroes*
- ▶ *Great Quotes from Great Leaders*
- ▶ *Great Quotes from Zig Ziglar*

To order call: 1-800-CAREER-1 (1-800-227-3371)

Other best-selling audio/video programs by Brian Tracy

▶ *Action Strategies for Personal Achievement*
(24 audios / workbook)

▶ *Universal Laws of Success & Achievement*
(8 audios / workbook)

▶ *Psychology of Achievement*
(audios / workbook)

To order call: 1-800-542-4252